SCOTT, FORESMAN FIRST TALKING STORYBOOK BOX

A is for Alphabet by Cathy, Marly, and Wendy

Anatole by Eve Titus

Angelo the Naughty One by Helen Garrett

Benjie by Joan M. Lexau

Chicken Licken

Frances Face-Maker by William Cole

Harry the Dirty Dog by Gene Zion

Humbug Witch by Lorna Balian

Jack and the Beanstalk

Little Bear's Pancake Party by Janice

Mickey's Magnet by Franklyn M. Branley and Eleanor K. Vaughan

Mother Goose Rhymes

Over in the Meadow by John Langstaff

Straight Up by Henry B. Lent

The House That Jack Built

The Little Rabbit Who Wanted Red Wings by Carolyn Sherwin Bailey

The Shoemaker and the Elves

The Tale of the Flopsy Bunnies by Beatrix Potter

Timothy Turtle by Al Graham

What Mary Jo Shared by Janis Udry

Where's Andy? by Jane Thayer

The Shoemaker and the Elves

Illustrated by D.G. WHEELER

Special Scott, Foresman and Company Edition
for *Scott, Foresman First Talking Storybook Box*

Once upon a time there was a shoemaker who was very good at making boots and slippers and shoes. Even so, the shoemaker and his wife were poor. At last one evening the shoemaker noticed that he had only one piece of leather left. He could make only one more pair of shoes. Then his leather would be gone.

The shoemaker's wife said kindly, "You are tired tonight. Why don't you just cut the leather and go right to bed? Tomorrow you can do the rest of the work. You can sew the shoes and nail them together. If you make a very fine pair, maybe some gentleman will pay a lot of money for them."

The shoemaker thought that his wife's idea was a good one. So very carefully he cut a pair of shoes from the last piece of leather. After the pieces were all cut out, he put them on his workbench. Then the sad little shoemaker and his wife went upstairs to bed.

The next morning the little shoemaker rose very early. He ate breakfast, and then he went to his workroom. There on the workbench was— not just pieces of leather, but—a handsome pair of shoes! The shoemaker was so surprised and so delighted that he called to his wife, "Come quickly and see the wonderful thing that has happened! The shoes that I cut out last night are finished. Come see how well they are made."

The shoemaker's wife ran to the workroom. She, too, cried out in delight. "These shoes are the handsomest shoes I've ever seen! Surely someone will pay a very good price for them."

The shoemaker's wife proved to be right. Before the morning was half over, a man came into the shop and tried on the shoes. They fit him perfectly! The man paid much more than the usual price because he was so pleased to get such a beautiful pair of shoes.

The shoemaker was pleased, also. Now he had enough money to buy leather for TWO pairs of shoes!

That night the shoemaker cut out the shoes and laid the pieces on his workbench. "Tomorrow," he told himself, "I will make TWO fine pairs of shoes." He and his wife were feeling much happier when they went to bed that night.

Again the next morning the shoemaker found that his work had been done during the night. Instead of pieces of leather on his workbench, the shoemaker saw a pair of boots and a pair of dainty slippers for a lady.

Later that same day a man and his wife came into the shop and bought the boots and slippers. And now the shoemaker had money enough to buy leather for FOUR pairs of shoes.

Again the shoemaker cut out the shoes
before going to bed. And the next morning
FOUR pairs of shoes stood gleaming
in the workroom. The shoemaker sold
these shoes and bought enough leather
to make EIGHT pairs.

Day after day the same things happened,
and soon the shoemaker and his wife had
lots of shoes in the shop and plenty of money
to live happily and well.

One evening the shoemaker's wife said,
"I certainly would like to know who has
been making all those beautiful shoes
for our shop. Whoever it is, has been more
than good to us. Let's stay up tonight and
see if we can find out who has been making
the boots and shoes and slippers."

"All right," said the shoemaker. "After I
finish cutting the leather, we will hide behind
the door. Maybe we CAN find out who has
been making the shoes for us."

So the shoemaker and his wife hid behind
the door to the workroom. Just as the clock
struck midnight, two elves hopped through
the window into the room. The two tiny men
hurried to the workbench, picked up the leather,
and began to make shoes. They sewed and
hammered and hammered and sewed—one pair
of shoes after another.

In what seemed like the wink of an eye, the shoes were all finished. Then the elves danced twice around the room, hopped up on the window ledge, and disappeared into the night. The shoemaker and his wife had never seen such a sight!

As they went up to bed, the shoemaker turned to his wife and said, ''Those elves were the fastest workers I've ever seen. They have made us rich and happy. Can't we think of something nice to do for them?''

The shoemaker's wife said, "Did you notice the clothes that the two elves were wearing? Nothing but little short pants that were all ragged and torn! Those elves need some warm clothing. I'll make shirts and new pants for them. I'll sew a jacket for each one, and I'll knit some stockings."

"And I'll make leather shoes for their feet and hats for their heads," said the shoemaker. "It will be OUR turn to surprise THEM."

The shoemaker and his wife set to work. They worked all the rest of the night.

The shoemaker and his wife sewed and knitted and hammered all the next day.

It was evening again when the shirts and pants, jackets and stockings and hats, and two tiny pairs of shiny leather shoes were finished.

The shoemaker left no pieces of leather on his workbench that night. Instead, he left the clothes for the elves. Then he and his wife hid behind the workroom door once more.

Just as the clock struck midnight, the two little elves leaped into the room. They ran to the workbench, then stopped in surprise!

The elves stared for a minute at the clothes lying there. Then they quickly put on the shirts and pants, jackets and stockings and hats. Last of all they put on the shiny new shoes.

The elves were so happy that they did
a dance on top of the workbench. Next they
jumped to the floor and skipped and hopped
three times around the room.

As the shoemaker and his wife watched
from behind the door, the elves finally danced
to the window, hopped up on the ledge, and
disappeared into the night.

Much to their sorrow, the shoemaker and
his wife never saw the two elves again. But
with all the shoes they now had in the shop—
just waiting to be bought—they never had to
worry, either. So the little shoemaker and
his wife lived contentedly from that day on.

They often talked about their friends,
the elves. The shoemaker's wife would say,
"I wonder where those fine little elves
are now."

And the shoemaker would say, "I wonder.
But you can be sure of this, good wife,
wherever they are, they are helping
someone else."